About the Author

RUTH L. SCHWARTZ was born in 1962 and spent her childhood and early adulthood moving around the United States. She left home at age sixteen, received her B.A. from Wesleyan University and her M.F.A. from the University of Michigan, then settled in the San Francisco Bay Area in 1985. She worked as an AIDS educator for many years, and has taught creative writing at Cleveland State University and Goddard College. She teaches at California State University, Fresno.

Schwartz's first book, *Accordion Breathing and Dancing*, won the 1994 Associated Writing Programs Award and was published by the University of Pittsburgh Press in 1996. Her second book, *Singular Bodies*, won the 2000 Anhinga Prize for Poetry and was published by Anhinga Press in 2001.

Schwartz has received fellowships from the National Endowment for the Arts, the Ohio Arts Council, and the Astraea Foundation. Her other honors and awards include two Nimrod/Pablo Neruda Awards, two Chelsea Awards for Poetry, the New Letters Literary Award, the North Carolina Writers' Network Randall Jarrell Prize, *Kalliope* magazine's Sue Saniel Elkind Award, and a Reader's Choice Award from *Prairie Schooner.*

EDGEWATER

The National Poetry Series was established in 1978 to ensure the publication of five poetry books annually through participating publishers. Publication is funded by the late James A. Michener, the Copernicus Society of America, Edward J. Piszek, the Lannan Foundation, the National Endowment for the Arts, and the Tiny Tiger Foundation.

2001 COMPETITION WINNERS
Betsy Brown of Minneapolis, Minnesota, *Year of Morphines*
Chosen by George Garrett, published by Louisiana State University Press

David Groff of New York, New York, *Theory of Devolution*
Chosen by Mark Doty, published by University of Illinois Press

Terrance Hayes of Pittsburgh, Pennsylvania, *Hip Logic*
Chosen by Cornelius Eady, published by Viking Penguin

Elizabeth Robinson of Berkeley, California, *The Tunnel*
Chosen by Fanny Howe, published by Sun & Moon Press

Ruth L. Schwartz of Oakland, California, *Edgewater*
Chosen by Jane Hirshfield, published by HarperCollins Publishers

EDGEWATER

POEMS

Ruth L. Schwartz

Perennial

An Imprint of HarperCollins*Publishers*

HarperCollins books may be purchased for educational, business, or sales promotional use. For information please write: Special Markets Department, HarperCollins Publishers Inc., 10 East 53rd Street, New York, NY 10022.

FIRST EDITION

Designed by Nancy Singer Olaguera

Library of Congress Cataloging-in-Publication Data
Schwartz, Ruth L.
    Edgewater: poems / Ruth L. Schwartz.—1st ed.
        p.   cm.—(The national poetry series)
    ISBN 0-06-008253-4
    I. Title. II. Series.

PS3569.C56738 E34 2002
811'.54—dc21

                                                        2001051932

07 08 09 ❖/RRD 10 9 8 7 6 5 4 3 2

Acknowledgments and Thanks

I am grateful to so many, for so much:

Most recently, these poems—and my life—have been enriched by the love and perspicacity of Marianne Dresser and her dog Bodhi.

My friends Alison Luterman and Julia B. Levine helped me enormously, as always—both with the work of making life into poems and the work of letting life be life.

My mother has always valued the poet in me—a rare gift to receive from a parent, and one I deeply appreciate.

Jane Hirshfield's generous and clear-sighted editorial suggestions led me to make this collection much stronger.

Along the way, I was befriended, stimulated, challenged, encouraged, enlightened, inspired and/or graced by Nin Andrews, Diana Bilimoria, Héctor Carrillo, G. Jill Evans, Ginny Gibbs, Lisa Grigg, Jane Mead, Renee Nank, Jean Reinhold, Thrity Umrigar, and Bruce Weigl

For their contributions, both witting and unwitting, to particular poems, I am indebted to Wendy Fremstad, Ted Lardner, Adam Nobel, Lynne Page, Emilia Paredes, Tim Seibles, Sisters Dhammadinna and Jotika, the Lindsay Museum, and the Sterling & Reid Brothers Circus.

I'm also thankful to the following Ohio institutions and individuals: the Ohio Arts Council for a grant that helped to fund the writing of many of these poems, the Poetry Forum, the Butcher Shop, the Antioch Writers' Workshop, and my colleagues and students at Cleveland State University.

My colleagues and students at California State University, Fresno, have continued to provide me with inspiration as well, and I thank the College of Arts and Humanities for a grant that helped me travel to India.

This book would not be what it is without the observant, tender, sensual, and seeking spirit of Kim Rose.

Last but not least, places and animals are also muses for me. The spirit of Edgewater Park, a beach on the shores of Lake Erie in Cleveland, Ohio, infuses this book. I'm deeply appreciative of the insects, birds, dogs, fish, and other life-forms that make such frequent appearances in my world, and in my work; I don't know how I could be a writer without them.

Previous Publications

The following poems were previously published (many in
earlier versions):

"Important Thing"   ATLANTA REVIEW

"Fetch"
"September, Edgewater Park"
"After You Held Me in Your Hands, Circling My Skin with
    Rivers of Touch, Training All the Blood in Me to Follow"
"Edgewater Park"   CHELSEA

"Proof"   CHESTER H. JONES PRIZEWINNERS

"The Swan at Edgewater Park"
"Failure"
"Aliens Can See Us Now"   CRAB ORCHARD REVIEW

"Millennium Love Poem"
"After Columbine"   NIMROD

"This Monkey"   PATERSON LITERARY REVIEW

"Figs"
"Letter from God"   PRAIRIE SCHOONER

"Lautar"
"Why We Drive Highway Five
    in February"   SOUTHEAST REVIEW

"Dog on the Floor in the Pet Food Aisle"
"Cleveland, March"
"Still Life"   THE SUN

Contents

Fetch

Nothing is ever too hard for a dog,
all big dumb happiness and effort.
This one keeps swimming out into the
icy water for a stick,
he'd do it all day and all night
if you'd throw it that long,
he'd do it till it killed him, then he'd die
dripping and shining, a black waterfall,
the soggy broken stick still clenched
in his doggy teeth,

and watching him you want to cry
for all the wanting you've forsworn,
and how, when he hits deeper water,
his body surges suddenly, as if to say
Nothing could stop me now—
while you're still thinking everything
you've ever loved
meant giving up some other thing you loved,
your hand, the stick stuck in the air,
in the shining air.

Edgewater Park

Even now, at the end of the century,
when our survival as a species

seems a matter of dumb luck,
our bodies studded with these jewels of tenderness

the way so many dying insects
bead the spider's web—

even now, on the cliffs above the beach,
I see two men who meet for pleasure,

nothing else,
fully clothed, in a cove of bushes,

standing face to face, as if to dance—
but one has both hands on the other's cock

and is pulling at it, tenderly—
and the body, at least, would name this *Love,*

and who are we to contradict
the pure animal body?

All around us, in expensive houses,
men and women married many years

touch far less joyfully than this,
with less attention to the hunger of it.

And truly, what do we have left
but moments of this gazing, pulling

at each other, at ourselves,
the shells ground finer and finer

under our feet,
making a kind of jagged sand,

the insects we call *Canadian soldiers*
rising from the water in great swarms

to mate and die—
on my window they looked like tadpoles,

hundreds of them flooding toward
the light—

and some of them
made their way in,

the whiteness of the ceiling
became their water,

they massed there as full of joy
as if it were the sea.

By morning they were dead,
their many bodies

light and dry,
littering the tabletops.

And the spiders, lucky spiders,
ate for weeks.

EDGEWATER

Talking to God on the Seventh Day

You're not so sure about this world?
Listen. Take another look:

                    the joyful reckless
barking dogs, convinced of doom, hysterical,
or only proud to own the yard,
the block, the wind—
                    the raised welt of their voices
roughening your dreams.

The new leaves slightly bent, like
                    fingers on guitar,
rippling their chord of twigs—
and the still-bare
slingshot branches,
      naked as the tails of rats,
liminal as roots.

The squirrel crushed in the road,
      its tail still
waving, in the wind of
passing cars, a flag,

and the blackest of black crows,
      breaching the body
with its surgeon beak—

black needles of its feet so pleased
with death,
     which is also meat, and life.
Another squirrel, its rapid jaws

          muttering around a nut:
          My number not up yet not yet bub not yet—

Now tell me why you ever thought
you could improve on this

          music, this hunger.

After Columbine

The lake lit not like glass, but like
the torch which moves along
the underside of glass,
burning a hole in the sky, between the dusky clouds.
Now a dark airplane flies right through it.
Down on the beach, a man is throwing sticks
into the water:
for each swollen wave, a stick,
for each stick, a wave,
as if he means to set right
some critical imbalance . . .
Yesterday, on Hitler's birthday,
says the newspaper,
kids in Colorado opened fire
on other kids, killing thirteen:
the worst school massacre this year.
I did it 'cause you were mean to me,
one of the gunmen said.
Opened fire:
as if it were a box, now cracked,
consuming its own lid and hinges,
sparking out, unstoppable,
into the tender,
flammable world—
this world where *gunmen*
is a compound word,
as if the men and guns they held
had fused somehow, turned into some new animal,
limbs like rifle barrels,

damaged human heart.
Meanwhile it's sunset on the lake, I'm likely
not safe here, the path is darkening,
but each wave breaks a different way, and the great
body of the water
is blue-green as the eyes of someone
I once loved.
That man down there throwing his sticks,
the seagulls shrieking overhead
as if to urge him on—isn't he tired yet?
But no, the water opens each time differently
around each stick, the way our bodies open
every time we love.
The lake is beautiful, there is no denying it,
the clouds, the plane which enters them,
the helpless blaze of sky,
the man whose arm is half a windmill, energy itself,
the arc of it, the purity of effort.
Even the tongues in our mouths are beautiful.
Even the words we speak, not understanding.

December, Edgewater Park

The beach is covered with feathers, but the gulls
lining the edge
between the dun-colored sand and the pewter

rolling mirror of the water
don't seem to be missing any—
they can afford to lose what they lose,

to shit where they will, to drink and fish
from the shitted water,
assailing hunger with the whiteness

of their perfect breasts, high flight:
incontrovertible, their seagull lives,
certain of everything.

And while the water rolls in, and the wind rolls farther,
while the feathers float and skitter
down the longing body of the shore,

we who also believe ourselves
the very center of the world
keep on parting and embracing,

burying ourselves
in gritty living mounds—
then kicking up great sprays of sand,

brushing off our tender skin
to begin again.

Bodies at Work

We are watching three enormous elephants
lie down willingly on their massive sides.
Elephants who roll like dogs,

rise on their heels like begging dogs,
squatting on their redwood legs,
holding out majestic paws—

watching them rise with astonishing grace
onto the forests of their feet,
watching as the middle elephant,

led by a trainer in sequin bikini,
begins to sway its hide to a flamenco beat.
The great sad proudness of the body,

mute absurdity, the proven grace of it.
Also the silent gravity of touch.
Also the second elephant, hooking the sinewy tip of its trunk

into the slender rising ribbon of the first one's
tail, the third
into the ribbon of the second's tail.

Meanwhile women in bright silks,
skirts the colors of crepe-paper roses,
yellow violet, pumpkin violet,

flip and bend, flashing their skirts high—
(the teenage girl behind us hisses, *they oughtta
be ashamed of theyselves*—)

now the skirts are gone,
carried from the ring like wilted blossoms;
now ropes have lowered themselves from the sky;

the women
            begin to climb.

Ashamed? Of what?
Doesn't every one of us
dream of living in those bodies?

—in the necessary sweat beneath their arms,
in the coiled hungers of their cunts?
There in the bodies at work becoming

more than themselves,
while also remaining, like the elephants,
            relentlessly themselves . . .

Loops through the air, forward and backward flight.

Pond Beside the River of Kings

The leaves in the mud are shattered wings.
The cracks in the mud-covered rocks
are elephant skin.
Who threw down, cast off those wings?
What wants to be born
from this exploding skin?
The red dog wades and splashes
in dank loveliness.
Tiny mosses, ferny hands
sprout all along the path.
New frogs sing opportunity—
We are, we are—
in the heart's tree.
Can it be true, O wide gray world?
Do you love us now?

Millennium Love Poem

1

    It's nineteen ninety-nine, and two strangers talk
via computer,
                arrange to meet,
                to fuck.
Heads of mountain goats, their fantastically curved horns,
impassive faces, marble eyes
call the light to places on the wall
in the Wild Game Inn,
                where our two are practicing
a different sport. *Bodies bodies bodies* say the newspapers,
but they mean the dead—
           Kosovo, Sarajevo,
           Palestine.
Here in Cleveland, we're still fucking
as if it could save the world,
or us within it;
we want everything
and nothing, digging through the body
like an earth, with our naked hands.
           Outside, Spring takes over
with a great thick chirping, ecstasy
of building, feeding, dizzy twirling
mating of the birds
in the still-bare trees.
           I sell lumber, says the man. *Hardwoods.*
Oak, birch, ash . . .
           And the woman thinking: *Ash, after all,*
is what we come to.

They are not young, have learned to navigate
this maze which is their flesh.
They know the curves, the pace, position
of the fingers which will make them feel
            what they long to feel;
earnestly they try to teach each other.

2

Strangers arrange to meet, to fuck,
except they call it *making love*—
                        as if love could be assembled
from materials at hand,
the way a sparrow builds a nest,
beaking bits of twig
and plastic, threads and grasses
to the chosen place,
            which shudders now, in the wind,
on its old hinge . . .

                        A man enters a store
from the gusting street,
muttering about trust,
how there isn't any,
and 'cause of that, he says, I'm gonna have to
murder all of you,
in your *beds*—
            and then leaves again.

Jesus, how we hate and crave
this clanking of one awkward heart
beside another.

3

And then the frogs gone mad with longing
in the first damp, after months of drought,

frogs on every inch of ground,
mating and singing and dying, and others
                       mating with the dying,

we have to move them with shovels
just to step outside,

                still they keep on singing.

4

Suddenly, without warning,
                the daffodils spring up,
rows and rows of buttered swaying,
fluted cups held to the light;
the trees erupt in blossoming,
                every flower an explosion!
                every flower an explosion!

—after every disappointment, every failing of the shattered
will, the nerves, the tongue, the brain, the heart

5

Sometimes our bodies melting together, your legs, mine,
your big head against my chest, next to the hole the universe
keeps rushing into and out of, I remember a friend said,
after her failed suicide:
It isn't happiness which saves us,
only curiosity.

I wanted to see what came next.
Sometimes we hear a shot, then a scream,
then, seconds later, the chiming bells
from the old clock tower,
then, for whole moments,
silence.
Now, through the window,
a woman folding sheets,
bringing the clean white corners together,
holding them to her chest.
Through the floorboards, someone else's
sweetness—two human voices together,
rising, rising.

6

The sheets, in yet another bed
in another motel, on another highway,
always white and stiff, as if to scold the pliant,
sweating flesh
of the ones who rest, or try to rest,
love or try to love, enclosed by these four walls,

this fabric bleached and starched and dried, ill-
fitting as the body, stretched to house the soul
through all its wanderings,

the clock ticking beside the bed,
no, not ticking, glowing, its implacable lit face
like a smaller, fallen moon,
disappointed, but still keeping time,
the way we always keep it, leaching out
invisibly inside us,

the Vacancy sign flashing on and on,
the Bible, always the Holy Bible,
the way the human heart still beats.
Still we twine our bodies, letting them say *love*

and *you* and *now,*
placing one hand on the crook
of the other's elbow, angling one cheek
toward the other, wide and tender blade,
still we move like magnets toward the center
of each other—we do this over and over, we can't
     stop doing it—

between the simple crosses of the old graves,

against the lonely ocean of horizon.

Pondering the President's Semen on the Intern's Dress While the Screen Door Creaks

Everything swells which is wooden
It is like the flesh, creaking open all night, unlatchable
A veces el cuerpo pide, said the man on the boat
Sometimes the body asks
On the upper deck, still clothed,
I leaned so he could take me from behind
We sailed between islands jeweled with iguanas
And rare nesting birds
Male frigates, inflating enormous red necks
Boobies, dancing hours of courtship
On their blue feet
Once, two giant tortoises,
Their prehistoric bodies locked in place
The guide whose job it was to tell me
About natural life
Mostly wanted to know what an American
Whore would do, and for how much
He asked the way others had asked how much
It cost to eat lunch in my country
Many who spoke no English
But had memorized the names of American cities
Philadelphia, they cried out fervently, *Chicago*
There are no words which tell the body's hunger
It is not one cell in the wood, but all the cells
Which make the door unclosable

Why We Drive Highway Five in February

for Marianne

1

Just to see that many trees
burst weeping into blossom:

stung with tears white
as white rivers, pink and fierce

as babies' fingernails,
yellow stamens proud with pollen, blooming

like they'll never stop—
while those black handkerchiefs, the crows

fold and unfold themselves
in the upper trunks,

as if they've come to blot out grief
with blackness, or to worship it,

to lift it with their black black wings
oiled by the sunlight between storms,

fly it far up into the always-
                holding sky . . .

Meanwhile, the fat wise cows against the fence.
The herded tenderness of sheep.

Meanwhile, great swathes of mustard and lupine,
sprawl of openmouthed yellow and purple.

Meanwhile, your voice:
I love you. How did that happen?

(It happened, says the world,
like this,
and this,
and this.)

2

The tender triangle of skin
beneath the throat, between the collarbones,

where your age shows first—
the cross-hatching of the fabric of skin

like cotton faded, pinked,
overwashed, worn thin—

tiny window of flesh foretelling
the coming failures of flesh,

sweet dream of flesh unguarded
as the flayed and lovely heart:

revivified, relentlessly exposed.

3

The great white egrets in the grass—
each of their bodies an elegant *S*
posed like a stalking, snatching proof
of beauty in this world.

Who placed them here?

And who placed into us
this love?

What force loved us into love?

4

The rows and rows of identical trees—
those branches still disguised as dead,
these branches riven now by life and light.

The swaddled bodies of the cows,
their raw-rubbed teats.

The fields and fields of sheep, stubbled rough as stones.

The way we turn off the car and tremble, for a flicker
of a second, in the humming silence, before pushing open
   the doors.

II

Sunday Night at Edgewater Park

My fragile messy species half-
undressed for the cool love
     of lake water.

Proud-bodied girls with shorts wedged high,
boys strutting skinny naked chests,

their ribs outlined as delicate
as spines of autumn leaves,

a frail old man whose t-shirt reads
Ex-Teenager,

all lowering themselves into the wet,
the wanting dark.

We've strewn the beach with styrofoam
like sorry petals pulled from some corsage—

so many prom queens' white gardenias
littered, like our best intentions,

over everything.
Yet even so, in the late heat,

the water parts to let us in,
yielding like our flesh

for other flesh.

Picnic

Now the sun rides bareback
on our necks again,
returning us to the colors of cockscomb,
ruffling the fields in rows of gladness
after summer rain,

now the tomatoes
fill us with gladness,
basil splays its spicy anise-
perfumed leaves for us;

peaches break apart
in our hands,
each half an aureole of sweetness;
purple figs ooze gladness
from their purple rumps;
the cream swirls in our coffee
like a cirrus cloud.

And while the birds cut open
the vast plains of sky
with the dark scissors of their wings,

while the birds sew shut the sky
with the dark-feathered needles
of their wings,

we have the drying but still green
grass tangled through my fingers
like your hair,

we have your hair between my fingers
black and soft as grief,

we have the narrow stream,
the bottom-loving carp,
the orange of their tails and fins—

we have this breeze
like a dream of a breeze,
we have my dress pulled up,
my bare and heated thighs.

EDGEWATER

Lautar

(traditional Gypsy singer)

1

    The voice is broken like a knotted string
    being pulled slowly from the mouth,
    catching,
            for an instant,
    on each of the knots.

    There is a storm in it.

    There are sheep in it, which have discovered
    the edges of cliffs.
    Their hooves tender, their bodies
    unimaginably soft
            as they fall.

    The voice is disturbing.

    Our lives are disturbing.

    There is a whistling in it,
    faster than breath.

    There is a frantic haste toward joy
    like a woman's finger on her clitoris
    circling harder and harder.

    There is a sound of drums and clapping,
    something which might be pulled from us,
    something which fears the pulling.

A pulse between the breasts
which rises up to protest the voice.

Then a finger
laid against the lips,
hushing us with longing.

2

The lips and finger,
their knowledge of each other
sensual, impassive,
like the bodies of two people
who do not remove their clothes
yet lie down together, dumb with need.

Two people in a field of snow,
their bodies melting up from it.

A field where sheep
lie where they fell,
stubbled in their fleecy white,
their broken-open red.

3

It is good sometimes to listen
to what breaks us open.

This pressure in the throat,
this pressure in the chest,
this pressure in the clitoris
                which we have rarely spoken of—

for who among us does not yearn
to hear their own name sung?

September, Edgewater Park

We've come here to read about love
carved in stone—
Mark -n- Joan 4-ever,
Wayne loves Tammy, 1990—
          a caterpillar noses briefly
through these etchings of devotion
to your mortal palm—
then back to the sweet cracks
between the lovers' names.
This slate is soft enough to hold us,
hard enough to bear our scars.
Over our heads, the trees,
unbroken green—
only a few already stippled,
tipped with red and gold,

the way our softest skin, near forty,
creases us, the way the water folds
onto the stony shore.
Once, past darkness, on this beach
I watched a man playing accordion,
rocking the battered instrument
on his big belly, lungs of song
shutting and opening—
and how he fingered forth the notes
through all the years of losses in his hands.
The taste of fall is in us now,
crisp apple, sweet late corn,

and every night, the way the sunset
burns and burns along the length of us,
the way we burn, so fiercely,
every time we love.
Sometimes, when the waves coast in,
they don't know where they've been.
Sometimes they seem a little puzzled
as they break, with all the gladness
of water, against the rock.
Still they go on rolling, supple, shining
like the newly born.

On the Way to the Airport

The moth we found in the rain was almost
as big as a hand,
immobile as a hand laid down
in supplication on the wet street,
but when you touched it
it moved a little,
stilted and arthritic, or in shock, or
partly drowned,
you nudged it to your palm
and it held on—
its thin feet grasped surprisingly—
and opened out its double wings
with their embroidery
of blacks and browns.
It waited in your hand
like a smaller hand,
neither trusting nor defeated,
neither with fear, nor the absence of fear,
as if it had simply arrived at the end
of what it knew.

There was rain between us, and your leaving,
the hard black leather of your thrift store
jacket, with its broken zipper,
the way it stiffened your soft shoulders;
over it, your lips, which my lips
touched like twins—

we who were also at an ending
of the world we knew,
waiting in all our helpless separate
tender dignity—
to be beaten down, or drowned, or lifted up.

Touch

The skin
and the serious organs beneath it
cannot help themselves; we rise
to our own surfaces

in small, daring, dazzled blips
like the fat spring frogs which pause
between the leaves of watercress
and mint—then dive

kicking deep again. What if we could
transform like that? you ask, as even fatter tadpoles
waddle, wiggle legless selves

through the water's
waiting skin. Or maybe we can,
you answer yourself. Fervent
as we are

in this incarnation,
in this ardent flesh.

Oh God, Fuck Me

Fuck me, oh God, with ordinary things,
    the things you love best in this world—

like trees in spring, exposing themselves,
    flashing leaf-buds so firm and swollen

I want to take them into my mouth.
    Speaking of trees, fuck me with birds,

say, an enormous raucous crow,
    proud as a man with his hand down his pants,

and then a sparrow, intimately brown,
    discreet and cautious as a concubine.

Fuck me with my kitchen faucet, dripping
    like a nymphomaniac,

all night slowly filling and filling,
    then overflowing the bowls in the sink—

and with the downstairs neighbor's vacuum,
    that great sucking noisy dragon

making the dirty come clean.
    Fuck me with breakfast, with English muffins,

the spirit of the dough aroused
    by browning, thrilled by buttering.

Fuck me with orange juice,
    its concentrated sweetness,

which makes the mouth as happy as summer,
    leaves sweet flecks of foam like spit

along the inside of the glass.
    Fuck me with coffee, strong and hot,

and then with cream poured into coffee,
    blossoming like mushroom clouds,

opening like parachutes.
    Fuck me with the ticking

clock, which is the ticking
    bomb, which is the ticking heart—

the heart we heard in the first months,
    in the original nakedness,

before we were squalling and born.
    Fuck me with the unwashed spoon

proud with its coffee stain—
    the faint swirl of a useful life

pooled into its center, round as a world.

Ohio Highway

As if I'd failed to love, and needed
to be shown again:

the birds falling like darkened snow
to the fertile ground,

the birds flocking like lovers' hands
to the damp of green.

Green of the highway median,
narrow planted strip of life—

while on the heated current
rising from the road,

three red-tailed hawks angle their black
bodies through the sky,

their hunger certain,
hovering, transparent—

and all of us humans in cars on the highway,
maybe eighty miles an hour,

braiding our way through painted lanes
in a kind of dance,

sometimes the semis honking
to keep the beat,

and at the overpass—it's raining now—
two longhaired teenage girls on the bridge

waving to the steady passing
of the cars—and I think they think they love us

like an ocean, like we love anything
larger than us,

which goes on in spite of us,
utterly apart from us:

the rain like longing made visible,
filtered through the sieve of sky;

the birds which, any way they fly,
are always flying home.

The Snake

for Kim

It's an actual snakeskin, not a metaphor:
the living snake long gone
in its fine new diamond skin,
leaving behind this onion emblem,
proof of passage, transformation—

and because I love you, I caress
its stretched and crackling gems.
Its emptiness.

There is no longing left in it.
It held what it was meant to hold.
Like your hands: which travel

from the handle of the knife,
breaching the spine of fish—
to dirt, to trees, to the sweet figs
untwisting holy from their twigs—
your hands, their kinship to my skin

impossible to replicate, deny, or keep—

your hands, faithful to nothing
but themselves—which is to say,
as faithful as the snake:

leaving, relinquishing,

gleaming over and over
into the world.

The Sky at Edgewater Park

I walked as far as I could walk. Then I walked farther.
Across the miles of graying water. I sat on a log,

on broken shells. A few fish flopped on the unhealthy water;
others, eyes and mouths wide open, lay against the tide.

The seagulls disdained them,
chattering whitely. I tried to open wide

the jaws of love. The sky which had already stormed
lay placid, far above the water. The water gurgled

and relinquished. I sat on a log half-stripped of bark.
I saw the wings of fish, the fins of feathers shifting

on the sky. I remembered fish at home
in my freezer, potatoes blooming purple eyes,

the bread and the butter to spread on the bread.
I remembered hunger. The moon came out,

three-quarters of a gleaming plate,
and birds sang toward it in the night trees.

I knew my longing to hold you completely
was like wanting to cradle the moon

in my palms: the desire was not wrong,
only unattainable. I knew you would go on waning

then waxing inside me again, if my love grew large enough,
like sky. I did not know why the fish had died,

but I touched them, their silvery scales in my hands,
full of the lake which bred

and was the death of them. I touched my hunger
gratefully. The sky held everything.

Important Thing

I've always loved the way pelicans dive,
as if each silver fish they see
were the goddamned most important
thing they've ever wanted on this earth—
and just tonight I learned sometimes
they go blind doing it,
that straight-down dive like someone jumping
from a rooftop, only happier,
plummeting like Icarus, but more triumphant—
    there is the undulating fish,
    the gleaming sea,
there is the chance to taste again
the kind of joy which can be eaten whole,
and this is how they know to reach it,
head-first, high-speed, risking everything,

        and some of the time they come back up
as if it were nothing, they bob on the water,
silver fish like stogies angled
rakishly in their wide beaks,
—then the enormous
        stretching of the throat,
then the slow unfolding
        of the great wings,
as if it were nothing, sometimes they do this
a hundred times or more a day,
as long as they can see, they rise
    back into the sky
to begin again—

and when they can't?

We know, of course, what happens,
they starve to death, not a metaphor, not a poem in it;

this goes on every day of our lives,
and the man whose melting wings
spatter like a hundred dripping candles
                    over everything,

and the suicide who glimpses, in the final
seconds of her fall,
        all the other lives she might have lived.

            The ending doesn't have to be happy.
            The hunger itself is the thing.

Grapes

What I wanted
were the grapes—hanging in dusty
rounded pubic triangles
from their knot of vines.
So I don't know who held you
in that narrow
dormitory bed,
who stroked your hair
with all its foreign magic
until three a.m., wanting
infinity itself.
Who was it
in my body then?
I could say *longing*
or the Spanish word, *anhelo*—
just saying it: a halo in my mouth,
the sound of *oh,* tongue curling and alive
as a hooked fish.
I could watch people drinking wine,
their glasses clear and lovely
as the afternoon,
their stems so long and thin, each hand
must cup a globe,
fingers holding up its heft
from underneath, lit curve of breast,
liquid sweet as mercury
falling and rising in the palm.
But I know Fate
must hold us this way,

never touching,
only tipping us,
so when I think of you,
it's strange—
that headlamp glare I held you in,
that eagerness
to forsake everything.
As if, once having seen such light,
the eyes imagine they could close
forever, gratefully.
As if the end of longing were a place
we could arrive,
kick off our boots, sit down to supper,
bread and soup and wine
—and plates and plates of dusky grapes,
droplets of water caught and glistening
on their bluish skins.

One Life

Sometimes the sadness
circles back,
rocking you far

from any future dreams—
back to this one cold
day, this car,

to what this dog was
when it died,
here, on the highway off-ramp,

curled in its dark
well of fur,
openmouthed, its teeth

a rainbow of white stones.
You don't know why
its lips draw back like that,

what it saw, or why nostalgia
never yields,
or what it is you want most

in this world—
only that your cells hold on,
alert as dogs,

pricking and burning,
bright and hot
as the lit horizon.

Aliens Can See Us Now

(*Weekly World News* headline)

Right now. At the duck pond. One human per table,
while the fountain arcs its narrow
streams like a hundred little-boy angels, urinating

constantly and gracefully
onto tiny floating boats of bread.
The air is thick with crumbs, we're sad, a little envious—

watching the ducks in their duck lives,
squabbling, murmuring through grasses,
rising on the water, flapping, bellowing, incontrovertible.

We're here, the man wearing three hats,
reading his newspaper out loud.
The woman with an empty cup,

sucking for hours at her straw.
Big-bellied watchman, handcuffs chiming,
eyes above the uniform, above the American

flag on his shoulder, pale and soft
as a soft-boiled egg.
How small the aliens must find us,

murmuring and flapping
through our human lives.
How sweetly we distract them

from their cosmic sadness.

From 30,000 Feet

All around me, toppled strangers
sleep like children: undefended fortresses,

open mouths. There are mountains traveling
beneath us, massive folds of bodies

robed by snow. I could count a thousand trees,
delicate fringe round the mouths

of lakes; from here it is suddenly clear
how many roads there are,

how they lead everywhere; the slopes appear supple,
endearing; the cities too, elaborate and harmless,

the cars industrious as ants,
the red roofs of the tiny houses,

turquoise swimming pools like stones
set into the jewelry of the world.

I can't see pain from here; I can't see you, my far
darling of darlings—not your need of me,

not your need to be free of me. From here,
I think, I can love you like water,

beautiful and speechless in its tides.

After You Held Me in Your Hands,
Circling My Skin with Rivers of Touch,
Training All the Blood in Me to Follow

Some of the branches bear no signs,
but on others, tiny revelations—
odd furled reddish leaves
like a newborn's fists.
We didn't know we were doing wrong,
we only wanted, as the poet said,
to weep and love—
I mean that weeping which is the body,
the currents linking every flesh
to every stone,
every water-striding insect's
graceful jointed legs
to our own fingertips.
And love, the kind which leaves us begging
as the briefly-dead have begged,
after returning to the bodies
in their hospital beds—
they could be craving
life or death,
it doesn't matter which—
wanting anything that badly
is a kind of grace,

the way a dog will brave the biggest
rush of water, over and over,
just for a stick—

not just any stick,
but the one we threw.

The beach is littered with the others,
pale and smooth as bones.
Spring now, and this strangeness.
The branch doesn't intend to bud;
it can't understand what love
has done to it.
The dog leaping and leaping
on the sand
with that same fever.

Proof

Spring comes slow and late in Cleveland, so we learn to look for
signs: the yellow hard-sheathed head of daffodil
which has been visible for days, but won't unfurl—
and then a loosening, as if one lock had come undone,
        a single curl of promise.
We humans, we can't feel Spring coming,
so we sulk and mumble, numbly wait;
but the black-throated sparrows are different,
they've built a nest already in an opened hinge of window,
when I look up I see tail-feathers, sitting and sitting on that
  wedged-in
pile of sticks, saying *faith* and *faith*,

and tonight on my way home, outside a brick apartment building,
suddenly, a row of pansies! Such familiar
speckled faces, openings of purple, freckled gold,
and a man standing beside them, pointing,
and the woman he'd brought there, gazing
at the flowers, saying *proof* and *proof*,

and I turned the corner into the sun, that bright
        setting sun which blinds us
sometimes, in our failings, in our grace.

Failure

Every day, the sun going down
against the industrial skyline,
the cellophane windows of warehouses,
the puffing laboring pillars of smokestacks,
the living trees bare-armed, disguised as dead—the sun
   going down
is still the largest thing we have ever seen,
and its unlikely orange-pink
still emblazons the horizon
like the revelation of the body.
It is frightening to be almost 40
and still believe I would die without love,
although no more or less so
than it was at 16;
also, no less true.
We fight over whether you love me enough,
and my headache all day is a horizon
wrapped too tight.
Meanwhile, my mother's teenage son
is burning up for love.
Because he is half my brother, I half understand his flesh;
I want to tell him there's no rush,
this need will still consume him
fifty years from now.
Instead I lie in bed, tending my own flame.
With age, we work at wanting no more
than what we have, and always fail.
The sun going down reminds me we must
keep failing, it is the only thing worthy
of our bodies.

At the Wildlife Rescue Museum

The bald eagle on the terrace,
chained with shiny silver to his perch,

surrounded by the white stains of his shit
like a scant snow,

staring at nothing, or at you,
his dark fierce iris swum in gold,

might rather be dead.
But finds himself alive instead,

in Purgatory, ringed by glass and steel,
the endless gaze of human animals,

each meal of limp mice handed up
with heavy glove.

It seems an equal treason if he eats
or does not eat.

Still, the hunger claims its own,
parting the sickle of his beak.

Daily at 12:30, for an audience.

Oakland Sky After a Week of Rain

The whole enormous song of it, stretched without complaint
over the sage of bay,
over the hunched silence of the cormorants,
their monk-like silhouettes against the edges of the docks
holding their wings absurdly wide, awkwardly waiting
   for the world
to make them dry, so they can dive, then wait to dry,
   then dive.
You say you love me, and you do, and still so much
keeps us from touch,
the light falls so heavy on us it makes us dark,
the puddles gape like mirrors in the ruined streets.
I say I love the truth, and I do, though often I think it will
   wash me away
in its wholly indifferent impassive and righteous flood.
Meanwhile the heart drums its desire—despair—desire,
as if those were the only notes which made it beat.
Meanwhile the cormorants in water,
slick with speed, unstoppable—
helpless on land, doomed to this soaked embrace.
And so they wait. We wait.
Sweet heart, sweet wrenching heart, it isn't wrong to want
what you don't have,
but neither is it wrong to love
what lies in front of you—the way the sky contains
   so many crevices
which hold and do not hold back the escaping light,
the vast and shaken landscapes of dark.
Look down: the black necks of the geese

devoutly bent to praise the ferny newly-sprouted grasses
with a snap of beak.
Look up: a startle of pigeons, their bodies
the color of untouched plums—
rising into a stubble of stolen white.

Sandusky

Under the pink light spreading out
over the bay with its unruly ache,
its ravaged bodies of styrofoam cups,
its limbs of rusted machinery—and still
the leaping of its fish,
still the rippled circles of their breath
under this pink light,

you showed me pictures, I showed you pictures,
our faces in front of the various houses,
our hands in the hands of the various lovers, and I thought
if this is all
we will ever be—

this water sluicing foam and wild
over the mossy broken piers,
the way the waves crack open and,
in the same instant, form themselves again—

this bruise of melons, garnets, rubies,
bruise of late light sinking
to its knees—

if this is all we will ever be,
poured into, held and married by
this perfect, disappearing sky,

it will be enough.

Sunset at Edgewater Park

The sun casting a long haze down the water:
long bright broken gleam, narrow tower
falling toward me—if I were a fool
I would think it gold, dive to try to hold
its possibilities. If I were a god I would walk
its wobbling path. But the Jet Skis bounce right over it,
glup, glup with their ravenous engines
and then move on.
Small, human, we step into the water,

our skin tentative and greedy, water
thirsty and impassive—
the stench of it, the scent of us,
craving something large enough
to hold or drown us. And here we have found it.
The beach is small and dirty, like our lives,
the water polluted, finite, yet its hunger
boundless, like our own—
tide stroking up against the stones,

lovers' fingers in each other's hair.
No wonder some of us roar out
across the sun, across the sea
like Moses in the year 2000, brazen, motorized.
O we are fools sweetened by longing, as angels
are sweetened by taking the form
of shrieking gulls—their piercing gluttony, their soiled,
perfect wings.

IV

The Swan at Edgewater Park

Isn't one of your prissy richpeople's swans
Wouldn't be at home on some pristine pond
Chooses the whole stinking shoreline, candy wrappers, condoms
    in its tidal fringe
Prefers to curve its muscular, slightly grubby neck
      into the body of a Great Lake,
Swilling whatever it is swans swill,
Chardonnay of algae with bouquet of crud,
While Clevelanders walk by saying *Look*
    at that big duck!
Beauty isn't the point here; of course
    the swan is beautiful,
But not like Lorie at 16, when
Everything was possible—no
More like Lorie at 27
Smoking away her days off in her dirty kitchen,
Her kid with asthma watching TV,
The boyfriend who doesn't know yet she's gonna
Leave him, washing his car out back—and
He's a runty little guy, and drinks too much, and
It's not his kid anyway, but he loves her, he
Really does, he loves them both—
That's the kind of swan this is.

This Monkey

25 CENTS—THE MONKEY JUST TAKES THE MONEY
50 CENTS—BETTER VALUE, HE SHAKES YOUR HAND
ONE DOLLAR—SHAKES YOUR HAND AND KISSES YOUR THUMB
—Carnival Sign

This monkey sits
in the very middle
of Middle America:
stars and stripes on every porch,
neat grass, clean streets, the town parade—
If You Love Your Freedom,
Thank a Veteran—
earnest students puffing saxophones,
lovely girls in A-line skirts
bearing pom-poms like exploded blossoms.
Right here, in the carnival center of town,
the Ferris wheel, the Tilt-A-Whirl,
pink cotton candy lofting toward us,
corn dogs held up like little flags—
this monkey sits
in the middle of everything,
his small, partly human face
creased, like ours, with desire and weariness.
And it's true, he reaches toward us
with the tiny fur-ridged fingers
of one tiny hand,
over and over he takes our coins,
slips them into the tiny pocket
of his tailored vest—

It's a real monkey, the barker cries—
over and over, like a good machine.
And we line up for this lost wilderness.
We gaze into his looted eyes.
We pay and pay for him to shake our hands,
to kiss our naked thumbs.

Not only the words, but the bodies we have

fail to reveal us. For example, Ben
in his dark-eggplant skin, his bruiser frame,
ripple of muscle, *wouldn't want to meet him*
in a dark alley some night,
is actually tiny, scared;
there's a III after his name, he comes from some kind of
pride—but that didn't stop the beatings,
electric cords, my mother's shoes, he says.
        What can be made of this? Ben
tries hard, sits next to me in class,
reads out loud, mispronounces words,
apologizes for having told me
more than I should have—and I, small, white,
shake my head,
I'm the teacher, as invisible to him
as he is, mostly, to me,
this is the fog we—all of us—are in,
stumbling in our separateness,
as if our shame and hunger made us
anything but twins.
By the time we turn toward each other, it's dark—
and isn't it always an alley?
        When you talk to me,
        when I listen,
always narrow as that first journey, forced that first time
to the world's wide light,
the first of a billion perilous, separate breaths.

Introduction to Poetry

Before class, in my car outside, I write:

I do not know if God lives in these trees
turned into standing fire,
or in the waving flicker of their hand-shaped leaves,
or if there is a different god
in every leaf, a thousand gods
golden and falling—and a few
stray gods still green,
others red as devils' robes—
or if God lives in the disappearing
blue of the blue sky,
bright as an eye, and big enough
to cry for all of us.

And after class, I write:

The cheerful perky pug-nosed blonde
who has, until now, written nothing but rhyme,
tonight read aloud
in a steady voice
a poem about her "drunk-ass father"
who, before he passed out on the couch,
said *I could fucking kill you all*
and hide the bodies
and no one would know—and,
when I praised the vivid language, said proudly,
It's a real quote.

Outside, in my car, I write:

There are those who say Christ died for us.
These leaves, do they fall
in the service of life?
How hidden we all are.

This

for Tim Seibles

> The autobiography of the Unabomber, who had a
> girlfriend only once in his life, speaks again and again of
> what he calls his "acute sexual starvation."
> —*Time* magazine

If I could write a poem about love,
I'd have to start with the years of thinking
it meant being someone else,
the years of trying to figure out who,
trying to invent the face,
the body, the laugh . . .
So when I read your poem of longing
for the woman with long thighs,
recalling the pulse of her cry when she came,
I wonder for a minute how to change the sound I make
when *I* come—until I remember, love
creates the body
which is more than just a body; love is what turns
pulse to song,
song to the moment when we know ourselves
alone—
    and then slide deep
into the other, as if each lover
were a downhill road
to the center of that winter river
where I lay once on a flat, sun-heated rock,
the water gathered around me like glass,
the snow nearly blinding me

when I looked toward shore.
When I make love to a woman,
I never want to stop.
Maybe it's the same for you.
When she lets me, really lets me,

rocking up against my hand
like it's a world
I'm pushing into her—and pushing into her
becomes a world,
a place where I can land the lonely
ship of my body, plant the flag
of my fingers, kiss the soil—
where I can never live.

If I could write that poem, I'd have to
say how badly I've wanted to live there,
abandon the cold brightness
of my life onshore,
swirl myself inside the puckered
current of another,
as if that way I could save them from drowning,
or they could save me.
                    The truth is,
we will not be saved.
All our perfect appetites,
our stubborn praise
will not be enough.
                    The truth is
larger than salvation.
In the shifting flooding times,
our lips take root against the melting

river of the other, and the body
      knows,
no matter who we are, no matter
who they are—

      we were born because of this,
      we were born for this.

In India

1

Here's a man whose legs below the knee curl into smoky
tendrils of flesh, who pedals his wheelchair bicycle

with his hands; and here you are, with your excess of limbs,
trying to fit yourself against the body

of your lover. The sweat which coats your skin in bed
is also the river destroying the road,

willful helpless froth churning the land to ruin—
while giving suck to crops, unrolling lush green tapestries:

ravage and redemption in a single swell.
Here's the problem of love, and its desolation;

here are the leper's tiny scalloped
palms—all of her fingers are gone—

clasping together the coins you give her; and
here's your lover, asleep now, with daylight

splashed over her cheekbones, spreading
to her forehead, stopped by tender hairs.

Sometimes it seems wrong to love one person
and not another—to love one *instead* of another,

though you tell yourself it is all you can do; more light,
beam polished like an apple, shines on her uncovered

shoulder; her arms are defenseless in sleep, like a swimmer
held still in the water; bare, nestled like newborns;

her mouth slightly open, her breath slowly keeping beat.
As long as she sleeps your eyes wander

the kingdom of her; we are always beautiful
when we sleep, when what is hard or frightened in us—

they are the same thing—reverts to unconscious grace.

It is monsoon. It rains as if the world
were only rain. When it stops, the streets are raw and clean,

even the mud is clean in them; even the sky seems
exhausted and grateful, its grief turned into such a flood

you could strip off your clothes and bathe in it.
The road is disappearing; its stones are being pried loose,

hurtling downhill to land in other rivers;
later they will be gathered, chopped by hand,

lofted on women's heads;
brought somewhere else, to do some other work.

2

After your fine meal, you package up the food;
in this country where people are hungry

in the streets, you say, it is wrong
to leave bread on the table—

your waiter smiles indulgently at this.
You carry the food out into the street,

you mean to eat it later; when the girl in dirty rags,
holding a baby in her arms,

approaches you, points to the food, and then
her mouth, her stomach, then her baby's mouth,

you say No. Walk faster, make your body rigid,
slide your eyes away.

(In your heart there's an old leper
whose fingers are gone, who holds up stumpy

lumps of palm, whose pain is visible;
in your heart there's one who sometimes

gives to her—though never too much.)

Passing at night by rickshaw through the old city,
where men sleep in their splintered carts,

you see one, wearing only underpants,
splashing his body—each perfect limb—

in a common fountain. It isn't a lie to say he glistens
with muscle and promise, with not-yet-vanquished

possibility. No lie to say love still might save you,
if anything can; nor to say you will turn away

often; you will falter, fail. The rain will fall. The roads will vanish,
stone by stone. Your heart will flood. Somewhere a field will grow.

Still Life

So: the heart opens in the chest,
wet like the tinsel branches of the palm tree standing
                    tall in sun
after rain, after a day so gray nothing could shine.
The heart shines; then it convulses,
longing, as usual, to touch and hold.
It expands and contracts
a few billion times—
that's what hearts do.
The palm tree
glitters for nothing and no one.
Stands through rain,
sun—that's what palm trees do.
You are too beautiful, the heart cries bitterly,
pulsing like orgasm around the gleaming world,
the monumental, never-to-be-grasped
beauty of the world.
The palm tree says nothing.
High, impossibly high in its branches
glow the ripened dates.

Figs

They tell us when they're ready for us, swollen round as
milk-filled breasts, their sides expanding, rippled, stretched,

oozing—no, weeping—the promise of ripeness:
opened like anus or cunt, mouth or eye,

a drop of honeyed sap from their bottoms
hardening like sweetened amber, offering, offering—

and then, when they are riper than ripe, souring on the tree,
fermenting vinegar inside their puffy skins,

inviting entry by small insects, blackly vigorous and winged.
The figs need wasps to burrow into them, to suck, to seed

and then to drown inside them, bursting
sacrificial filaments of light—

and we, to enter this same country,
need each other.

Cleveland, March

In the thawed and startled city,
in the center of the stream,
the white foam journeying so faithfully
around the stones and complicated roots
isn't clean—
still, the stems and spoiled leaves

wave gaily up in their decay,
the slimy moss grows slick as sex,
the bare trees hold aloft
the nudity of sky;
last winter's dried-up leaves, which had believed
all movement lost to them,

skip a little now, on the path.
You notice you are hungry, though not urgently.
You notice an old man on a bicycle:
how beautiful his face.
Also the bumblebee jogger in his yellow
t-shirt, tight black shorts;

the women striding with their small
deliberate weights;
the child wavering on skates,
each of her kneepads a smiley face;
several hundred gleaming ants
massed like a pile of spilled chocolate sprinkles

around the open mouth of a paper cup.
You are not crying about anything.
You are not even stopping yourself
from crying about anything.
Motionless in their red robes,

the robins meditate like monks.
A German shepherd, belly fringed
with tiny drips, squats shitting on the path.
The endless water thanks its endless
current, lucky as your life.

Mandala

Mica glitters on river sand;
ants carry each other's bodies

fiercely and without reason
over the small hills,

stumbling back- and forward, filled with
tragic gallant effort, going

nowhere at all—which is, of course,
where all of us are going.

The river is running, we say;
we mean the water moves like the

blood in our bodies, unquestioning;
we mean it catches hard on stone

and burbles upward suddenly,
white with song.

The stems of the low-growing blackberry bush
are scarlet—did you ever notice?

Its leaves are green and red, painted
by photosynthesis and death.

Its thorns are small, sharp and angled
like the soul made manifest:

pointing every way at once,
willing to bloody what they touch.

In the city, a team of monks
has worked for months

on a mandala,
dropping grain by grain

the pattern into place.
Such concentration in their fingers!

Mirrored steadiness of heart and mind.
Never a shirking; no thought of ease;

no leaning toward shortcut or compromise.
It must be perfect as they can make it,

which is to say, perfectly flawed as love—

When they have finished,
they will sweep it clean.

The Perpetual

All day long, outside my window,
        baby birds are pleading
and receiving,

squawking naked-headed open-mouthed
        and being fed;
all day long, the parent birds

fly back and forth,
        food in their beaks;
the grasses of their nest tremble with everything

the world can't stop.
        And who could bear a different view?
And who could fail to love such hunger?

O the lovely arc of need
        the body opens into.

Dog on the Floor in the Pet Food Aisle

It's so simple, really:
the tenderness we need
lives everywhere,
there is no place it does not live,

and we seek it
savagely,
and we flail and hurl and fling
ourselves toward the brass ring of it,
as if it were a narrow chance,
a shining and unlikely prize . . .

It is hard to pinch the air
between our fingers, but we are determined.
It is hard to survive by denying
ourselves, but we are accustomed.
It is hard to live inside the flawed
and gritty chambers we
believe ourselves to be,
but we have strapped our bodies in,
we watch our lives through airplane windows,
small and dim and scarred,

and even so, life noses up,
rolling before us
like a black dog,
its brown eyes steady as the sun,
its belly in the air, asking for touch.

Letter from God

I wanted to give you the swallow's egg, but it shattered,
Leaking yolk like joy. I wanted to give you the dead fish
But a bird had already stolen its eye. I wanted to give you
  the ruby socket
But the fish held tight. I wanted to give you the beach with
  its miles
Of brownish sand, mounds of bleached and broken shell,
But I changed my mind. I wanted to give you the trees with
  a little
Butter and lemon squeezed on top, but they were
  firmly planted.
I wanted to give you the slimy moss, the gnats like tiny
  exploding stars,
The driftwood crossed like mothers' arms. I wanted
  to give you
My hands, the morning bodies of dolphins,
Arcing easily from water, plunging in again. Hunger
And the absence of hunger. The willow trees bent low
  to the water,
The nippled peaks of the water, the living stone,
The names and hearts chiseled into the stone. Lovers say
  they will love forever
And in some other world, they might. In this world, a man
  on the boardwalk
Can write the entire Lord's Prayer on a grain of rice,
But everyone goes on running and dying
Like dogs on the beach, their bodies extended
Into forever, for nothing, for joy, for a stick.
I wanted to let you go but I thought I would die.

I wanted to let you live but you were already gone.
I wanted to sip you like fine wine, wanted to gut you
  like a trout,
Dip your delicate dripping spine
Like a holy feather into my mouth. I wanted South,
North, East and West. Wanted to praise you and catch you
  and throw you
Back, like one too small or one too beautiful
To keep. I wanted to marry you like the light
And then forget you like the dark. I wanted to promise you
  something, then give you
A thousand times what I'd promised, then take it away,
Then give it back again. There are sticks muscled as snakes,
Sticks never fetched, hopeless sticks. There are faithful
  sticks, and faithful
Mouths which carry them. There is a moon
  thin as Communion
Waiting to be dissolved on the tongue. There is a bluejay
In the tree, its feathers more dazzling than your veins,
There is a cardinal redder and brighter
Than your blood. Tongue of water, lip of water
Where two swallows mate like ribbons
Twisted into air.
This is it. Take it or leave it. Love,

Notes and Dedications

"Edgewater Park"
Edgewater Park is a real place, an actual edge, where Lake Erie meets the northwestern landmass of Cleveland, Ohio. It is also a mythical place, where any large body of water rests against the flesh of land.

"After You Held Me in Your Hands, Circling My Skin with Rivers of Touch, Training All the Blood in Me to Follow"
The line "We only wanted to weep and love" is from Tess Gallagher's poem "Trace, in Unison."

"Not only the words, but the bodies we have"
"Introduction to Poetry"
These poems are for my students, who entrust me with their truths.